Albuquerque Academy
Library
6400 Wyoming Blvd. N.E.
Albuquerque, N.M. 87109

D0471108

What's So Great about Cindy Snappleby?

Barbara Samuels

ORCHARD BOOKS   NEW YORK

Copyright © 1992 by Barbara Samuels
All rights reserved. No part of this book may be reproduced or transmitted in any
form or by any means, electronic or mechanical, including photocopying, recording,
or by any information storage or retrieval system, without permission in writing from
the Publisher.

Orchard Books, 387 Park Avenue South, New York, NY 10016

Manufactured in the United States of America. Printed by General Offset Company, Inc.
Bound by Horowitz/Rae. Book design by Mina Greenstein.
The text of this book is set in 16 pt. Gamma Book. The illustrations are pen-and-ink
and watercolor reproduced in full color.   10   9   8   7   6   5   4   3   2   1

Library of Congress Cataloging-in-Publication Data
Samuels, Barbara. What's so great about Cindy Snappleby? / by Barbara Samuels.
p.   cm.   Summary: Though Faye wants to be friends with the cool and confident
Cindy Snappleby, she won't put up with Cindy's calling Faye's little sister names.
ISBN 0-531-05979-0   ISBN 0-531-08579-1 (lib. bdg.)
[1. Sisters—Fiction.]   I. Title.   PZ7.S1925Wh   1992   [E]—dc20   91-17809

E SAM

To Nicky with love

One morning Faye gave every one of
her Betty-Sue dolls a perm.

"They look fabulous," said her little sister Dolores. "I think I'll give my Lulie a perm too.

"But first I'll brush Betty-Sue
Tennis-Pro's long, shiny hair."

"You know you can't touch my
Betty-Sue dolls," said Faye. "Certainly
not today. Cindy Snappleby is coming."

Faye went to the kitchen and brought out a tray with brownies and two glasses of pink lemonade.

"My favorite!" said Dolores.

"This is for Cindy Snappleby," said Faye.

Dolores scowled. "What's so great about Cindy Snappleby?"

The doorbell rang. It was
Cindy Snappleby. Cindy
looked Dolores up and
down.

"Faye, I didn't know your
sister would be home."

"Don't worry. She won't
bother us," said Faye.

"Little children can be
cute," said Cindy, "but
they're usually messy
and pesty."

Cindy strolled over to Faye's Betty-Sue dolls.
"I used to collect these," she said. "Now I think
they're overrated."

"Oh, those aren't mine," said Faye, blushing.
"They belong to Dolores."

"They do?" asked Dolores. "Then why can't I play with them?"

Faye ignored her. "Cindy, come to the kitchen. I made brownies for you."

After they ate, Faye and Cindy danced to their favorite group, Marvin Mellow and the Maniacs.

"I can do that," said Dolores.

"Dancing is a bore," said Cindy. "Let's play
jacks. I haven't lost a game in years."

Faye threw the jacks, picked up two, and
dropped one. "Oops," she said. "It's your turn."

"My friends want to know how I always win,"
said Cindy. "They're dying to know my secret."

"I want to know Cindy Snappleby's secret,"
said Dolores.

"It's very simple," said Cindy. "I'm steady
as a rock and cool as a cucumber. Nothing
bothers me."

"I have a secret too," said Dolores. "I want
to show Cindy Snappleby my secret."

"Don't bother us, Dolores. We're in the
middle of a game," said Faye.

"I promise not to bother you if you let me
show Cindy Snappleby my secret."

"Oh, all right," said Cindy. "It's the only way
she'll leave us alone, Faye."

Dolores led Cindy into her bedroom.

"This is my dollie, and her name is Lulie.
She's having surgery today," said Dolores.
"Is that your secret?" asked Cindy.
"No," said Dolores.

"This is my teddy, and his name is Dr. Leonard. He's doing the surgery."
"Is that your secret?" asked Cindy.
"No," said Dolores.
"I don't have all day," said Cindy.

"And this," said Dolores, "is…

Albuquerque Academy
Library
6400 Wyoming Blvd. N.E.
Albuquerque, N.M. 87109

HOWIE, TRINA,
AND UNCLE BOB!"

After Dolores shared her secret…

Cindy's game was not the same.

"YOU ROTTEN LITTLE WITCH," Cindy shouted. "I LOST THAT GAME BECAUSE OF YOU!"

"Now, get ahold of yourself, Cindy," said Faye. "Nobody calls my sister a witch."

Cindy grabbed her hat and coat and rushed
out the door.

"I NEVER, EVER LOSE A GAME
OF JACKS!" she hollered.

"There goes Miss Cool-as-a-Cucumber,"
said Faye.

"I liked it when you told Cindy
not to call me a witch," said Dolores.

"But what I liked best
was when you told her…

that all your Betty-Sue
dolls belong to me!"

Albuquerque Academy
Library
6400 Wyoming Blvd. N.E.
Albuquerque, N.M. 87109